My First Car was Red

For Rosa and Elise

Peter Schössow

My First Car was Red

Translated by Sally-Ann Spencer

GECKO PRESS

Grandpa brought me a surprise.

'For you,' he said.

It was rusty. Really rusty.
But you could tell what it was – a little car!
Exactly my size.

'Diesel or gas?' I asked Grandpa.
'Sweat,' he said.

That's Grandpa for you!

It was a pedal car.
It was *supposed* to be a pedal car.

Right now, it needed work.

So Grandpa and I got on with it.
First we took the whole thing apart ...

Then we hammered, sanded, patched and painted.
I chose the colour – shiny red. We drilled holes and
tightened nuts; we greased and oiled and upholstered.

We fitted new tyres that we found on the internet.

We couldn't mend the windscreen.
We had to have one made.

Then we put it all back together again.

At last it was ready.
Just like new.

'MY OWN CAR!'

It gleamed.
It looked so good!
It felt good, too.
It even *smelled* good – of fresh paint,
rubber, vinyl and oil.

I was happy. So was Grandpa.

'MY CAR!'

I was so excited.

Everyone thought my car was amazing. And I mean everyone!

I wanted to take it for a spin, but I wasn't allowed.

'Driving lessons first,' said Grandpa.

So off we went to Driving School.

Forwards, backwards, left, right.
Indicating.
Traffic lights.

Road signs.
Braking.
Braking in the rain.
Parking backwards.

When I could do everything, I got a certificate.

But Grandpa told me, 'Don't ever run over my bad toe again.'

Then at last I could go off on my own.
I'd planned the perfect route.

'Me?'

My little brother wanted to come, too.

'I don't think so. Driving is dangerous,' I told him.

'Me!'

'Who knows if I can handle it, let alone ...'

'Me!'

'In you get.'

'Go!' said my little brother.

I went. As I said, I'd worked out the perfect route.

My little brother wanted to go a different way.
I explained to him about backseat drivers.

'Turn!'

'It's my car! I'll decide where to ...'

'Turn!'

'I'm turning!'

'Turn!'

I turned.

We were off.
Straight through the village.

Past Granny Em's vegetable patch.
Past Farmer Erwin's horse.

'Hey there, horsey!'

We took a right at Granny Nola's.
(We haven't talked to her since
Mum's birthday. I don't know why.)

We sped along the track.

I overshot a corner and
had to reverse.

That's when the trouble started.
Something fell *plop!* on the ground behind us.
A wasps' nest had dropped from a tree!

'Go!'

It was an accident, but the wasps didn't care.
They were angry. They went for us.

'Go!'

I put my foot down.

We raced along.

'Go!'

We were going really fast, but the wasps were faster.

'Go, go!'

I swung off the track.

The terrain was rough, but it didn't slow the wasps.

'Go!'

They were right on our tail.

I pounded the pedals.
The wasps followed.

And then ... wet grass. Wet grass is slippery.

We weren't driving.
We were sliding ...

'Go!'

... away down a hill.

'Stop!'

I tried to brake ...

'Stop!'

... but I couldn't.

We kept going.
The wasps were still after us,
but not as many as before.

'Go!'

We were heading downhill.
Faster and faster.
So fast I didn't have to pedal.

'Go!'

So fast I couldn't use the brakes.

The wasps gave up.

'Stop!'

We were headed straight for a cliff.

'Hold on!' I shouted.

My little brother just said,
'Uh-oh.'

We survived the cliff, but then we shot into a tunnel.

'Dark,' said my little brother.

'Yes,' I said.

'Birds.'

He hadn't seen a bat before.

We shot out of the tunnel, into a paddock of bio-swine. That's what Uncle Ludwig calls his organic pigs.

(Grandpa says, 'Organic? Everything is organic!' That's Grandpa for you.)

'Stop!'

'Tree!' said my little brother.

'I know!'

'Tree! Tree!'

'I know! I know!'

'Tree, tree, tree!'

'I know, I know, I know!'

'Forest!'

Yes, a forest.

We hurtled through it.
Leaves, berries, toadstools and pine needles
pelted our helmets.

'Stop!'

I wasn't keen on the forest.
I had the feeling we were being watched …

'Stop!'

We were charging towards a creek,
with no bridge in sight.

'Stop!'

I tried to stop …

We took off.
We flew through the air.

'Whoa!'

And then ...
We landed.

I don't remember landing.
I just remember thinking, 'Uh-oh.'

When I came to, my little brother was bending over me.

'Dead?'

I lay there thinking, 'Oh boy.'
My arm really hurt.

'No, I'm not dead. But my arm really hurts.'
'This one?'
'Yes.'
'Kiss?'
'If you must.'

It seemed to work.

'What happened to the car?'

'Dead.'

It took us a while to drag the car out of the creek and head for home.

We pushed, and I worried.
'What shall we tell Mum?'

'Bambi!' said my little brother.

'Bambi?' Not a bad idea.

When Mum asked how it went, I told her about the baby deer and she seemed pleased that we'd missed it. 'I'm glad you're home in one piece,' she said.

I was too.

That night my little brother came to my bed.
'Cold!' he said.
I pulled back the covers.

I was thinking up a new route.
'Tomorrow we'll turn right at the stream.'
'Bushes.'
'Bushes? Oh, the bushes along the track ...
We'll clear a path, then.
It's good we had helmets, isn't it?'

But Cornelius was already asleep.

Original title: *Mein erstes Auto war rot*

© Carl Hanser Verlag München 2010

Text and illustrations © Peter Schössow

A catalogue record for this book is available from the National Library of New Zealand.

Typeset by Spencer Levine, Wellington, New Zealand

Printed by Everbest, China

ISBN hardback 978-1-877467-68-4

ISBN paperback 978-1-877467-69-1

For more curiously good books, visit www.geckopress.com